SNOWY CURVES

A BBW Alpha Male Romance

Jolie Damman

CONTENTS

CHAPTER 1

Molly

The snow was piling up outside the bus. Snowflakes falling from the dark sky, giving Bridmosam a chilly and inviting look at the same time. Buildings had been decorated with all kinds of Christmas lights, shining and blinking under the full moon.

I could see my reflection in the window of the bus. I was heading to this jewelry store called Bridmosam Jewelry. Located in one of the most populous and wealthiest parts of town, I knew I wasn't supposed to be here.

I was supposed to be in my one-floor house, watching TV and texting my friends. I should be thankful they were still with me. I was in college, so making friends wasn't too hard. I just needed to keep going to the parties, and they trickled right in.

The bus took a sharp turn, sending me against the wall and window on my right side. It was empty, safe for me and the driver. He was of African origins, his belly huge and pronounced. The inside of his bus smelled of cheap beer and piss, but it didn't bother me much.

I wore a beanie, two thick jackets, with one of them capable of blocking the chilly effect of this part of the country's wind, and a pair of pants to make sure I wasn't going to die because it was too cold.

It was cold to the bone outside, though the inside of the bus did have its own heating system. It was electric, not making much noise while it kept going and going to the next stop.

Once it got there, I was going to slip out of it and then proceed to the jewelry store I'd been thinking about for the whole year. Mom and dad didn't know anything about this, but I was going to buy them a Christmas gift. Something that could cheer them up.

I knew they both needed it.

Since breaking up when I was just thirteen years old, their lives had been miserable. They didn't have many friends anymore. Lived in different parts of the town, also having to depend on rents to continue having a roof over their heads.

This part of the city looked like something straight out of a European fairy tale. No power cables visible, people perambulating on the streets with their jubilant families, fathers laughing, and moms making promises to their children about buying the most expensive gifts they could ever wish for.

They made me hope for the same one day, that it could happen to me too. But now that I was 22, I'd already kind of lost hope. Perhaps I was destined to live this way for the rest of my existence, being nothing more than a single woman without kids.

I wished to have a child one day, a baby to hold in my arms, but I didn't think it was going to happen anytime soon.

The old buildings that looked newer than my home, even though the latter had been built way after them, tantalized me to come to live here one day. My dream of a place to live in, though, was still Rio de Janeiro in Brazil.

I was aware of the high crime rates in the city, but they didn't make me feel worried about them too much. Not concerned enough to make me as much as consider the option of not going to live there.

I sighed.

I didn't have enough money for that anyway, so it wasn't like it mattered much.

The bus began to pull over, halting by the metallic and glassy structure that was its stop. The jewelry store wasn't too far from here, according to the Maps app on my phone. I didn't know this part of town well, so suffice to say I couldn't get anywhere without its data.

I slipped out of the bus, proceeding to the store. The strong, howling wind kissed my cheeks, making me dip my head and focus on the information on the screen of my phone. It was a little old already. It hadn't received a security update in months, which meant that soon I was going to have to buy another.

I rounded the corner of a building that sold expensive clothes for women, ignoring the clientele inside it. I wasn't a part of them. I was never going to be. The kind of items they sold in there was out of my reach.

Stepping to Bridmosam Jewelry some more, I couldn't help but look for shelter in one of the still open stores. Most shops had already closed for tonight, and the ones that were open didn't have many clients in them right now.

The wind was blowing too hard, kicking up my hair behind my head. It was making me feel as if it was going to begin to cut lines in my cheeks.

I surveyed the area outside the shop for some seconds, and when I determined that the wind was calming down a little, I stepped out of the building I was in. I didn't pay much attention to what it was, but it appeared to be another jewelry shop in this wealthy part of the city.

The place I was in was like some kind of corridor, though it didn't have a roof. It was beautiful, Christmas lights covering the façades of every building, with a huge Christmas tree in the middle of it.

I exhaled, rubbing my hands together when I reached Bridmosam Jewelry. The façade of the shop contained the name on top of the entrance, and it appeared to be almost empty. Not many people were visiting it right now, and the ones that were didn't even glance in my direction.

With snow covering some of my clothes, I did my best to shake it off me without looking like some kind of homeless that was invading their space. One of the desk attendants snorted, and the other frowned at me.

I could read their thoughts. What is this good-for-nothing-of-a-woman doing here? Does she think we're in the business of giving some of our items for free?

I ignored their initial reactions. It wasn't like they could refuse me, not talk to me and ignore me. They were going to be working here for who knew how long tonight, and I was a customer like everyone else.

It took me the whole year, but I managed to save up enough for the necklaces I wanted to buy for my parents. The model was an 18k Gold Pavé with their initials as pendants, and back when I discovered them here, they won me over.

It was them that I'd thought that I needed to buy them for my parents. They'd broken up, and this was my way of telling them I wished they could go back to being what they'd been before. I didn't know if by doing this I was doing anything substantial to make that happen, but I was more than willing to give it a try.

Plus, it had been a pretty long time already since I last gifted them anything. I visited them often, and I knew how much they loved me.

I proceeded to one of the desk attendants, her being the only one in here that was still available.

"Hey, I ordered two of your necklaces in January, I think."

"What's your name?" She asked, her hand proceeding to the keyboard in front of her LED display.

"Molly Parkinson," I responded.

She typed the name down on the keyboard, acting all professional and pretending she didn't mind how close to a homeless I looked like. Compared to the rest of her clientele, my clothes weren't in tip-top condition. They had some holes and looked worn, too.

Nothing I could do about that, though. I didn't have anything better to put on for tonight.

She bit her lower lip, saying, "I'm sorry, miss, but I think your order wasn't processed then. You'd made a reservation, right?"

My heart skipped a beat. She couldn't mean what I was thinking she was, right? I hadn't paid for them at the time, but still... I'd thought they were still going to have some of them. They had a whole collection of those necklaces at the beginning of the year. They'd even owned some with repeated initials.

This attendant had to be toying with me. She couldn't be telling me that all the effort I'd put in saving up enough money was going to be for nothing.

"Could it be that you're mistaken? I did make the reservation, and I don't think I wouldn't have noticed something odd about it if it had happened."

She typed my full name on her computer again, but all she did was to shake her head one more time, looking at me as if she was saying that she wished me to leave the store.

"I'm really sorry, but it's not here, and I also regret to inform you that we don't have those necklaces anymore."

"You gotta be-" I was saying, raising the tone of my voice. Some of the customers who were window shopping turned their heads to me, wondering what it was that was going on in the shop.

The gleam of disdain in their eyes was unmistakable. If they could kill me and get away with it, they'd do it. Just like in that Purge movie, or whatever it was called.

I drew in a short breath.

"Alright, guess there's no point in insisting on it," I said, turning around.

When I was going to step out of the store, with a swirl of different thoughts spinning in my head, a possible solution crossed my mind.

I hurried back to the attendant, who couldn't help but frown her eyebrows at me again. She was so hopeful I wasn't going to come back. It was sad more than anything, to be honest, that she couldn't be much richer than I was and still considered herself to be one of the 'elite.'

"Could it be there's another store somewhere in town still selling that particular type of necklace?"

"Is there a reason why you want that and not something else?"

"It's for my mom and dad. I thought they were going to like it."

"Ohhh, I see," she said, looking better composed now and less ready to sting me again with her words. "I don't think I know another store that sells them. You might have better luck just getting something else for them."

I gave her a small smile.

"Sorry, I really need those, and I guess I'm going to have to look for them somewhere else. Thanks for trying to help, though."

I turned around and hopped into the first bus that showed up. I had some ideas of some other jewelry shops that could have at least something close to the necklaces I was looking for, so I was a little hopeful.

Hopeful and having to hold back the urge to cry while I was still sitting inside the bus. It was lucky of me that it appeared when it did. I'd thought I would have to be now walking around the whole town looking for that Christmas gift.

And who's to say the price tag in another store would be similar? I needed to keep that in mind, too. If it turned out it was more expensive, then I guessed I'd just have to shell out some more money in the form of what was left in my credit card.

Didn't want it to come to that, but for the New Year, I needed to make sure I was going to get something nice for them. I didn't talk to mom and dad often, but I did keep contact with them... somewhat, and I wanted to make sure as well they could look at the new year as something worth a new try.

Worth mending their relationship together.

CHAPTER 2

Christopher

It's high time it stopped snowing in Bridmosam, I thought while pulling over my Rolls Royce Ghost. It was nothing too extravagant for this part of the city. One glance to the side was enough to confirm that to me.

Some citizens drove the latest Ferrari models, Lamborghinis, and Mercedes without a care in the world. Bridmosam was a pretty big city, with more than a couple of million people living in it, but crime rates in this part of it were still pretty low.

Criminals learned and were finding out that robbing people here wasn't worth it. The police and some other authorities kept their eyes peeled for anything and everything they needed to focus on.

Without them, this place would be a warzone.

There was the odd homeless sitting on the sidewalk, begging for food and money, but he didn't bother me. I just passed by him, hand sneaking into my pocket and then flipping over to his hat on the floor some coins.

It should be more than enough for him to buy something for the night, maybe a cheap meal somewhere else in town. He wouldn't be able to get anything here, that was for sure.

I tugged at my red tie, checking myself out in front of a window when I passed by it. I looked good. More than that, in fact. I looked sharp, spectacular, and ready to melt some hearts.

That young lady on the phone... I was pretty sure she was going to fall on her knees in front of me, begging to see my cock. She wasn't even going to think about anything else.

I had this date with her. I was pretty sure she was obsessed with me, but I was still a gallant man. I needed a gift to present her with to make her think that of me, too. Didn't want her coming out of our first date thinking that I was some kind of... guy that just wanted to get in between her legs and nothing more.

I shook my head, a soft smile showing up unannounced on my face.

Proceeding to the jewelry shop located not too far from me, I couldn't help but admire all the Christmas lights on the facades of the buildings. There was even a pretty tall Christmas tree at one of the squares in the distance.

That was where I was soon going to meet up with my date. Amanda... She looked like such a beauty, her hair straight and pretty black, big eyes, plump lips, and with curves on top of curves without looking fat.

That was just the kind of girl I needed to meet up with, and that's without mentioning she was around 10 years younger than me. I loved 'em pretty little flowers like her, always willing to date me and find out that I was way more than they could handle.

Still hadn't found a woman with whom I'd like to marry, though. I was too comfortable with how things were at the moment. Making money, being the CEO of my own company, not having to depend on my family anymore for anything, and the like.

I was living the life, no doubt about it.

I stepped into the store, ignoring some people crossing through the main double door. They were laughing and smiling, looking as if they were in a hurry to get to their destination. I brushed off some of the snow on my coat, and then proceeded to the woman standing behind the main desk.

This was one of the biggest stores in the whole city, and they should already have the gift I came here looking for. I'd ordered it online, so they should have no excuses for not having it here, if they didn't.

For the love of God, I hoped they had it there and hadn't fucked it up. I needed that gift now more than ever. I just couldn't come to the date with Amanda empty-handed. I wasn't going to allow that to happen.

"Hey," I said, halting in front of the desk. "I've come here for an order of mine. It's a Petite Marmont Leather Wallet."

"Your name, sir?"

"It's Christopher Sheppard."

"Just a sec," she said, typing my name on the keyboard and widening her eyes a little in confirmation when she found it on the display of her computer.

"I'm going to get it for you, sir. Gift-wrapped, right?"

"Yes, gift-wrapped," I confirmed.

It took her no time to come with a fancy bag made of leather. It wasn't too big, so I could carry it with my hand over to my car without a problem. It also looked favorably nice, making me think that Amanda was going to love it.

Just one more reason for her not to pretend she was difficult when spreading her legs open for me, I thought without smiling this time.

I took the bag with me out of the store, swiping my credit card before that to pay for the gift. The wallet was going to come in handy for someone like Amanda, who just couldn't help herself when it came to spending more money than she should.

I turned to the right, my ears perking up. I thought I could hear the sound of a woman crying... I guessed? I didn't know that for sure, but my protection and Alpha instincts kicked in all of sudden.

A woman in need of my protection wasn't the kind of eventuality I could ever ignore, no matter what was going on in my life, or hers.

I rounded the corner leading into the alleyway, not finding at all surprising that I was looking at a woman crying on the ground. She was sitting on it, or more like, spread on it. I didn't know her name, but she was such an undiscovered beauty.

Even more beautiful than Amanda, whose first date I was still going to have.

She was covering her face with her hands, weeping. I zapped to her, getting on one knee and wrapping her in my arms. She peeled her eyes open, turning her head to me.

She couldn't help herself, a gleam of hope and longing in her eyes. She was cherishing this. The last thing she thought that was going to come to pass here was a man like me coming to her rescue all of sudden.

I was nothing more than a stranger, sure, but there was no denying she thought I was her guardian angel, the one coming here out of the blue and wrapping her in his arms.

And under this cold and snow, she needed a man like me now more than ever.

"Why are you crying?" I asked, unsure if she was going to respond or not.

I was pretty sure she was mesmerized by me, but that still didn't mean she wasn't going to do the most logical thing and just push herself away from me. As with any other woman out here in this town, she was aware of the danger of meeting strangers in dark alleyways like this one.

I didn't expect anything different from her.

"I've been looking to buy these gifts, necklaces, for my mom and dad, but I can't seem to find them anywhere. They are all sold out."

"You didn't try to buy them online?" I asked, still keeping her wrapped in my arms and letting the heat of my body pulse to hers, feeding her all the comfort she needed.

It was almost love at first sight, making me forget about Amanda. I couldn't even remember that I was supposed to meet her in about half an hour.

"I couldn't find them on the internet. They are pretty cheap, I guess, for someone like you."

"I could take you to some shops I know. Maybe they have them still, depending on the kind of necklaces you need."

"They are 18k Gold Pavé Diamond necklaces, and they aren't too expensive, though I did have to save up some money the whole year for them."

I regarded her with some curiosity and a willingness to bring her into my life, wondering how she could put up with that sort of thing without having already gone crazy. She saved up money the whole year for that? Really?

"First, let's stand up, and then we can talk about that some more in my car."

She stood up with me, my fingers digging deep into her curves. My dick was beginning to stiffen in my pants. I had condoms with me in my pockets and everything I needed. I was supposed to go on a date with Amanda, after all, so I came prepared.

But just when we finished standing up, she pushed herself off me.

"Sorry, we shouldn't be doing this. I don't want you to think I'm hiding something or have some kind of ulterior motive."

She was so stunning, her black hair framing her face to perfection. Even though she was wearing a beanie, I could perceive the beautifulness of her hair.

And that's without mentioning the intensity of her hazel eyes, how she looked at me without thinking I was just some rich fuck she could have sex with. I'd had some Zoom calls with Amanda, and I could see it in her face how she thought I was an easy man for her.

Not this one, though, whose name I still had to ask her about.

"I don't think that you have, or at least I'm not worried about that," I said, stepping to her and brushing a lock of her hair to the side of her face. "You're not going to tell me what your name is, miss?"

She exhaled.

"It's Molly, but thanks for worrying about me." She turned her head then. "I need to go now."

"You're not going to ask me what my name is?"

She chuckled, her cheeks getting rosier.

"Alright, what is your name, my dear and overprotective warrior?"

I was the one who chuckled this time.

"It's Chris, though you're going to have to fight a little to learn what the rest of my full name is."

"Oh, I can do that, though... There's still the matter of the necklaces, and I want to make sure I'm going to have them before the New Year. I just want to see my parents smiling again."

I put my hand on her waist, leading her out of the alleyway. This was no place for someone like her to be, and she didn't object to me doing that. I was 36 years old and I had more experience with this kind of girl than I needed.

I knew when I'd be crossing a line, and when I wouldn't be, if either of those things occurred.

"You're making me think you're hitting on me," she said when I stopped in front of my Rolls Royce Ghost.

"I might be doing that," I joked.

"So... you're really going to take me shopping tonight, scour the whole city just for a pair of necklaces?"

"Hey, it's the least I could do for someone like you, and tomorrow pretty much the whole city will be closed. If we don't find them before midnight, you'll just have to go to your parents' without them."

She regarded me with a hint of happiness in her eyes, getting on her toes and kissing my cheek.

"Thank you. I didn't know there were still chivalrous men in the world."

CHAPTER 3

Molly

I couldn't believe it. I was seeing it with my own eyes, one of the most beautiful cars I'd seen my whole life. It looked like something I'd be seeing in this part of town alright, the shine of the metal enough to make anything I'd ever drive before ashamed of itself.

To someone like him, such a wealthy and powerful man, it was nothing. I was pretty sure that when he bought it, the price didn't even dent his fortune.

I wished I could marry such a man one day, though I was still pretty sure that was never going to happen. Guys like him, much older and richer than me, just didn't have eyes for women of my kind. They sought girls of his societal status, who were just as wealthy as he was.

Even now, even though he was looking at me with curious and lustful eyes, he kept telling me he had something more important to be doing. Maybe he had another girl he was supposed to be meeting.

Either way, I was here and now. I was supposed to be hunting for the necklaces for my mom and dad, and nothing more. I should be thankful Chris here was willing to waste his time with me doing that.

Still couldn't believe I'd been crying in that alleyway until he showed up. And what a gentleman he was for having done that. I didn't think there was someone that cared.

He opened the passenger's side door, folding out his hand.

"So, are you coming or not? It's getting late, you know."

"Yes, thank you. I'm not going to waste any more time. I need those necklaces before it happens that all the money I've saved up was for nothing."

"I'm not going to let that happen," he promised, opening the driver's side door and sitting on his seat. I glanced around, examining the interior of the vehicle. I could sleep in this kind of comfort and it would be better than lying on my bed for eight hours straight, when that could happen, that was.

More often than not these days, I just couldn't sleep for very long. Too much in my mind all the time, and very little time and resources to solve my problems.

"Are you going to tell me a little about yourself, Molly?" He asked, his eyes looking at me through the rearview mirror. Chris was such a gorgeous example of male anatomy, and even though he'd put on many layers of clothes for tonight, I could tell that he had the body of a war machine.

He was built like a tank. No wonder when he wrapped me in his arms, he made me feel as if someone had put on a blanket around me.

"What do you want to know?" I asked, brushing a lock of my hair to the side of my face.

"Nothing out of the ordinary. What's your job?"

"I'm a desk attendant at the Bridmosam Hotel."

"Oh, really? I didn't think you were. I've been there sometimes before, when I couldn't sleep for like a week."

"You're serious? You couldn't sleep for a whole week? Did something happen?"

He lowered his head, focusing on the road.

"Yeah, my mom and dad... They had a fallout with me. We still lived in the same house, or mansion, if you'd like to call it that. It was pretty big, so it had more than enough space for me and all of them."

"Why did you fight them?"

"They kept saying I needed to settle down with the right woman, that one of my cousins was much better than me because of that, and all of that bullshit. I couldn't take it anymore, so I let out all of my feelings."

"Oh, I didn't know. I'm sorry."

"It's okay," he said, smiling. "That happened when I was like 19, so ever since then I haven't talked to them."

I widened my eyes in shock.

"You haven't? I thought someone like you were still pretty close to your family."

"No... I cut all my ties with them. Just didn't see the point anymore. They thought I was a failure, so I decided to show them I wasn't."

"And you did that by building your own company?"

He nodded.

"It's called Bridmosam Logistics and it does pretty much everything. Anyone here in the city looking for a logistics solution comes to me."

"Wow, it's pretty impressive, then."

A moment of silence ensued, making me feel a little embarrassed about myself. I wished I could say to strangers like him I also decided to build my own company and make it run like one of the best enterprises in the world.

"You're not having some kind of financial difficulty, are you? I could help you. I could get you a better job."

His offer did strike me as interesting and tempting, but no. I couldn't accept it. I needed to find my own way.

"No, but thanks. I'd rather not bother you."

"It's no bother."

I shook my head.

"Still, we should focus on the necklace-hunting thing."

"You're right, though I have to ask... you still keep contact with your family, right? Like with your mom and dad, since you're hunting for their necklace gifts."

"I do, yes, and I love them very much. We're very different in that regard."

He chuckled. "You're right, and I gotta focus on the road now and on getting to that shop. Don't worry, we're going to find the necklaces you need."

I couldn't help but feel so thankful that he was doing all this for me. If he was out tonight, then I guessed he had something to tend to, or was going to meet someone else. That he was doing this was pretty telling of how much he cared about me. And I was nothing more than a stranger. I guessed he just had a pretty good heart.

His body, even hidden under his layer of clothes, kept tempting me to touch him. If only I knew him better, we could be doing that. I could be on his bed, caressing his abs, his wide chest, and then kissing his lips. I'd do almost anything right now to make that happen, if I could.

Chris took me to many shops, and when reaching the last one, I grabbed his arm and said, "You know, I don't think we're going to find anything in there. We scoured the whole city, but still couldn't find what we're looking for."

"Are you serious? I'm doing this for you."

His eyes exhaled a hint of seriousness I'd never before seen in a man. This mattered to him, quite a bit. There was no denying that. And he was doing this for my own benefit more than anything.

With me being nothing more than a stranger to him, could it mean he was doing this just for the chance of getting in between my legs? I could perceive the seriousness and also something else under his pupils, but still... I didn't want to think that was his plan all along.

I wouldn't mind if he and I did it, but that was not why I was doing this. I was doing this for mom and dad, and nothing more.

His hands settled on my shoulders as he finally said, "Look, you don't have anything to worry about. What needs to happen here, will happen. I'm going to find those necklaces."

"But... what if we can't find them?"

"Then, we're going to figure something else out. Maybe another gift, something better. I don't know. Let's leave that for when we have to worry about it."

"You're right. I shouldn't be so worried about that right now."

He smiled, his impossibly white teeth keeping me hooked to him. I wished, once again, I could kiss him right here and now, but the thought he was nothing more than a stranger to me kept me frozen.

His hand looked for mine.

His hand looked for mine.

And he grabbed it and then led me into the store, just like that.

My heart was thumping in my chest, like a speeding train. He took through me their rolling doors, and then to the desk attendant standing behind it. He was nothing more than a guy in his early twenties, black hair, clean-shaven, and skinny. Nothing out of the ordinary.

Nothing like the peace of hunk following me and leading this crusade to find a pair of necklaces. Doing that for someone he still didn't know well...

"Uh, hello? Is there something you're looking for?" The attendant asked, his eyes looking sharp as he straightened up his posture. He needed to look confident, no matter if he was about to end his shift and go back home to enjoy the rest of the festivities.

"Yes, we are. I'm looking for this kind of necklace, with the initials J and R. They are for my mom and dad."

"You know, I'm not sure we have those here still. They are quite popular this Christmas and New Year."

"Please don't tell me we came all the way here for nothing," Chris said, putting his hand on the glass of his desk with more force than he should.

He looked frustrated, possibly knowing he could find out he'd come all this way for nothing. I shared his frustration, but we really needed to give the guy standing behind the desk, who was the only attendant here tonight, some time to look for that for us.

"I'm going to go check it," he said, turning around and following a corridor that led farther into the building. My hand tightened around Chris', looking for that comfort that only he could provide me with right now.

I did have some friends, but they were all spending their 29th of December with their families. They didn't have time for me, nor did they care I was having such a tough time with finding the gifts I wanted for my mom and dad.

They were all good people, but there were some things I couldn't share with them at all. I did tell them about the necklaces, but I'd also told them that everything was under control and that I already had the money for said presents.

They all thought I was making good money as a desk attendant, even though that couldn't be any further from the truth. The truth was that working like that sucked, more often than not. The number of people I had to deal with every day that was nothing more than assholes wasn't something I could count using just my ten fingers.

That I'd met Chris tonight and that he was helping me with this like this was so lucky of me. I'd thought, back when I was crying in that alleyway, that I wasn't going to find the necklaces for mom and dad at all.

Now I had a chance to make that not happen.

The desk attendant returned to me, his hands holding... The necklaces I'd come here hunting for. They were as beautiful as when I'd seen them at the beginning of the year, shining under the bright LED lights of the store.

"Oh, they are so beautiful," I murmured.

Chris turned his head to me, asking, "So, it's really them. I almost feared we weren't going to find them here. Though, as I said, I'd just have bought something else for you."

"No, it's really them, and I'm just so happy-"

And then and there, tears streamed down my face. Noticing that, his eyes widening, Chris wrapped me in his arms again, pulling me to him. I let him do that and rested my head on his wide, powerful chest.

"Shhhh, shhh. No need to be crying here and now, and especially not in the middle of the store."

I still cried for some time, weeping a little too. But my noises were a little too soft, so the desk attendant didn't hear them. When I pushed myself off Chris, though, he was going to see the swollen region around my eyes and figure out I'd been crying.

Dammit. I couldn't believe I was making such a fool of myself right in front of the man that had become my crush. Chris, I meant.

CHAPTER 4

Christopher

I t was still snowing outside, snowflakes falling from the sky and adding thickness to the layer of snow on the sidewalks and the roofs of the buildings. The temperature kept dropping, which for me was just one more reason to keep hugging Molly.

She hadn't come out tonight with the most appropriate of clothes. She wasn't feeling too cold, I imagined, but she should still be wearing something better. I didn't know this woman at all, but I couldn't deny we shared an impossible to control bond the moment I first landed my eyes on her.

She pushed herself off me then, shaking her head and trying to hide her face with her hands. I turned my attention to the attendant again, whose eyes were wide in surprise. He was no fool. He knew Molly was crying, though he wasn't going to mention anything about that.

"How much are the necklaces again?"

"Uhh, let me check," he said, grabbing one of them and turning it in his hand until his eyes landed on the price tag. "Each is 499.99 dollars."

"I'm going to pay for them with my credit card," I said.

He put the credit card swiping machine next to me, and I swiped it through the slit, happy this thing was finally ending. And I was happy for one more reason, too. With me paying for her gifts, Molly was going to regard me even more highly.

Her eyes looked at me with surprise and love, finding this whole thing nothing short of unbelievable.

The attendant finished putting the necklaces inside their boxes, and then handed them to me in a fancy-looking leather bag. They were the perfect gifts for her mom and dad, and when she handed them over to them, she'd be making a dream of hers come true.

I was just happy I was a part of that, too.

I offered her the bag, saying, "Here they are, and don't take too long giving them to your mom and dad. I think they'd appreciate it if you take them to them right away."

She chuckled, wiping the tears off her face.

"You're right. I just... didn't think you were going to pay for them too. I mean, they were pretty expensive."

"Oh, please. 1000 dollars is nothing for me, and that's without mentioning I think you deserve that tonight as well. I know how much these necklaces mean to you."

The guy standing behind the desk cleared his throat, his face getting paler. He didn't think I was going to be hitting on her in here, of all places.

I just narrowed my eyes. What was that guy thinking? That this store isn't an adequate spot for me to be talking with the only person that mattered to me now?

He took a step back, noticing my displeasure. Good. He was going to keep it to himself. We still had more than enough time here until he had to close the shop as well. Once the clock hit midnight, then Molly and I would walk out of here.

Before that, though, he was just going to have to suck it.

Molly looked a bit more startled than she should be when she said, "I can't accept it. I've saved up money the whole year for them, and I can't feel like I'm taking advantage of you."

"My little darling, it's no taking advantage of when it's my own choice," I argued, wrapping her in my arms one more time and kissing her right here.

I wasn't forcing anything on her. I could see the look of lust and of how much she wanted this in her eyes. This whole time, she'd been thinking about doing this with me, sealing our lips together, and now it finally happened.

I could keep kissing her forever, the feeling of her plump lips pressing against mine unforgettable. She wasn't resisting this too, just kissing me more, and more and more, until she couldn't even breathe anymore.

I ended the kiss then, locking my eyes with her. If she somehow thought this wasn't going to work, then it would be no problem to me at all to just end it and pretend that it didn't happen.

"Are you feeling okay right now, Molly?"

"Yes, I'm just... flabbergasted and shocked at the same time."

"Well, don't be. I'm doing this for you. The gift, the trip to here, the whole crusade just to find the necklaces... I've been doing all of those things for you, and I just want you to know that. I'm following my heart."

"Chris, I don't even know what I should be saying," she said, turning her head away from me.

Cupping her chin, I turned it back to me.

"Don't worry. Follow your heart too. You have nothing to worry about, and soon you're going to be able to give the necklaces to your mom and dad, too."

She chuckled, and I kissed her one more time. It didn't matter to me what she did after this, as long as she kept kissing me. I'd even forgotten about Amanda again, and dammit, I needed to call her to tell her I wasn't going to show up for our date.

Then, if this beauty here accepted it, we were going to set up a date too. I'd like to get to know Molly better, feel the curves of her body, knead and grope them. With each passing second, I could see that she thought the same way.

Oh, the way she kept hugging me, moving her hands up and down on my back.

She needed me without all these layers on, no doubt about it.

I could feel the pulsing of her warmth, and it was bathing me with it. I was cherishing it, enjoying it, all the while kissing her lips more and more. I guessed it was a good thing we were the last customers in the jewelry store. Although, if there were more of it here, I'd still be doing this.

I'd keep doing this, feeding Molly all she needed from me.

The guy standing behind the desk couldn't do anything other than to continue staring at us. And he could keep doing that for as long as he wanted. I wasn't going to stop making out with Molly.

I'd found the right woman for me, the one mom and dad kept insisting about for hours and hours until I finally stormed out of their mansion. I was never going to come back there. Not ever again.

Molly ended the kiss once more, pushing herself off me. "We shouldn't be doing this. I think you're going to meet up with another person tonight, right? Maybe even another woman..."

"Oh, I was going to meet up with Amanda, but she doesn't matter right now. I only care about you, Molly."

"How... can you say something like that when you already promised Amanda you're going to meet up with her?"

"She's nothing more than a girl I met online. The real love of my life is standing right in front of me."

"But... I don't understand. How could you be saying that when you could also be lying?"

"I'm not lying. Why else would I be kissing you right now?"

And just as I finished saying that, I brought her head to me, kissing her one more time. It didn't matter what she thought about Amanda, if she suspected I was lying or not. I was going to prove to her she was wrong about that.

I wasn't lying.

I was kissing the love of my life.

Making out with her one more time, I couldn't help but slide my hand under her right leg, pulling it up. She whimpered, and I began to grind my body against her.

I had no idea where the guy standing behind the desk was now, but I doubted he was still watching this whole thing. If it were just Molly here and a lowlife nobody cared about, then he'd already have called the police.

But since it was me and her, well... He had to think thrice before even considering the option of doing that, didn't he?

Molly pushed herself off me again. Dammit, how many times was she going to keep doing that? And then pulled up her hand still holding the bag with the necklaces.

"I think we need to go. The store *is* going to close now."

That guy was still standing behind the desk, his eyes wide and his face, pale. Hearing that, though, he let out a sigh of relief.

I smirked, turning my body to him. "We're going to leave, but only because we need a more appropriate place for us. And don't report us to the police, okay? If you do that, I'll know."

He gulped, nodding. "U-uh, d-don't worry, Mr. Sheppard. I wouldn't dream of doing that."

"Well, good," I said, grabbing her hand. "Then that means I won't have to fire you."

I could fire him, without a shred of doubt. I wasn't an asshole or anything of the sort, but if he stood in my way, then I wouldn't have a choice.

I was walking out of the store with Molly, and even though I still had to call Amanda and tell her why I was a no show – the agreed-on hour of the date was long gone – I was thinking of the first only.

I was going to take her to my house, and over there we were going to have all the privacy she could ever need.

It was going to be grandiose.

CHAPTER 5

Molly

There was no point in pretending it wasn't happening. I was in his house, cherishing the wine he'd poured just for me. His dining room, the table peppered with candles, was so romantic. He'd put on a dark suit with a grey tie, and he looked even more striking now than he did before.

He'd even taken me to another store just before the woman behind the desk could close it. She'd looked displeased that we had been her last customers tonight, but I didn't care.

What I cared about was how this man, Chris, was doing pretty much everything right with me. The food his cooks had made for us was nothing short of exquisite, and even though I'd already had dinner before coming out for the necklace hunting thing, I was still digging into this food.

What was it called again? Spaghetti with Lobster Pomodoro. I could keep devouring this delicious meal again and again, until my belly was full.

The table we were sitting at wasn't too large, being of a round design. We were sitting at these fancy-looking wooden chairs. They looked like something coming straight out of the middle-age, of the kind one could find in historical castles nowadays only.

It didn't take us too long to finish the dinner, though, the maids sweeping right in to take the plates to the kitchen and clean them up. I linked my arm with his, smiling and giggling. During the dinner, he'd been making jokes.

And now he'd just finished making another.

He also looked concerned with something, his lips parting to ask me a question. "Molly, you're not supposed to be giving those gifts tonight to your parents, right? I don't want you to think I'm forcing you to be here."

"No, I'm going to take them to mom and dad later. There's no point in worrying about that, and just relax, you're not keeping me here against my will."

"Then, how about going to my bedroom where we could have a bit more privacy?" He questioned, as if he'd read my mind.

"I'd love that," I said, keeping my arm interlaced with his.

He took me then to the second floor of his mansion, my ears hearing the noises of the maids and the other workers in it working. Even though it was the middle of the night, they were still working.

I'd seen it when it happened. He wasn't forcing them to work. They could leave at any moment, though they still had their own dormitories here. They were being paid for the extra hours they were putting in here as well.

It was all good. Chris wasn't the kind of man one would ever like to cross paths with, but he was educated and responsible for the people under his protection and care. The maids and the workers sported huge, winning smiles on their faces as well.

They were all happy, and it couldn't be any different. When you're working for someone like Chris, you don't have many reasons to think your life is trash.

He opened the door, folding out his hand on the other side.

"Care to come with me into my bedroom, miss?"

"Of course," I responded, smirking as I strode into the space.

His bedroom alone made me think it was as big as my own house, and that was putting it mildly. It might be even bigger than the lot it was on.

His hands settled on my belly, musclebound arms wrapping around me again. When he rested his head on my right shoulder, kissing my neck, he murmured, "You're making me so obsessed with you. You're like a girl coming out of a dream of mine. I wish to live with you for the rest of my life."

"You can't be serious. We've just met."

"And, does any of that matter? I don't think it does," he growled, kissing my neck some more and making me squirm. He was relentless, making me wriggle some more, trying to break free of his possession of me, but that was a lot easier said than done.

His hand snuck down, beginning to unbutton the dress he'd bought just for me. The heating system inside his mansion was so top-of-the-line we could be in here, in his bedroom, without the need for any other layers on. It was as if, outside, the temperature was lukewarm again.

I was living the life, and if this worked, if Chris decided to go on with this, then I'd love to tell my parents that I'd finally found the right man to spend the rest of my life with.

"No, I guess it doesn't," I said, still squirming against his hold of me, his hand undoing one more button, and then another and another. He was freeing my body, grinding his hips against mine, making me feel his enraged cock pulsing against my buttocks.

I was living the life, no doubt about it.

"Don't pretend you're a difficult girl, Molly. I know you want this," he murmured, undoing the last button of my dress, and then peeling it away from my body.

Without the dress on, I felt a bit exposed, though not too much so. I knew that with him standing behind me like this, keeping his body in constant contact with mine, that there was nothing and no one I'd rather be with at this moment.

"You're making me blush," I moaned, turning my head to him and kissing his lips.

"Is that a problem?" He questioned, winking.

I didn't respond, letting his hands do his thing. He unhooked my bra, sniffed it for a second or two, and then tossed it over his head. "You're not going to need this anymore," he affirmed, kissing me one more time.

He tightened the hold of his arms around me, his hands cupping my breasts. They weren't small, nor were they necessarily big. I was still pretty impressed his hands were large enough to hide them both, though.

He wasn't applying much pressure, his muscles bulging and flexing. Most of my skin was touching his suit, making me beg him to take it off as well. I'd love to see him just in his underwear, allowing me to devour him with my eyes.

"You're going to make me think I'm making a huge mistake now," I moaned, feeling my legs weakening by the second.

"Again, I don't think that's a problem unless you really think it is. And if you think so, we should do something about it."

I giggled, his hands kneading my boobs and then pinching my nipples. "You're so hot and beautiful, my Queen," he murmured against my ear.

Just when I thought he had enough of that, he looped his fingers underneath the band of my pair of panties. Applying enough force and pulling it, he ripped it off me. I gasped, shocked at his show of strength.

It didn't matter that I was a bit more on the chubbier side. He could do anything he could ever want with me now, including sweeping me up in his arms and then carrying me to his bed.

His hand slid down, finding my engorged and hard clit. He flickered it a couple of times, saying, "I'm only going to continue this if you're okay with it. Otherwise, I'm going to stop, take you home, and never see you again."

"Please don't do that. I need you. Now, more than ever, I need you."

"That's what I thought," he cooed, kissing me some more, this time pecking my back and then my buttocks. Chris wasn't just loving my body, he was worshipping it.

I turned around, grabbing his tie. "You're not going to leave me at a disadvantage here."

"I didn't think I was going to," he said, letting me pull his tie and take it off him. I also tossed it over my head, tsking that it had taken me this long just to get rid of it.

"Allow me, then," I murmured, putting my fingers underneath his suit's coat, pushing both sides to the left and the right, and then taking it off him. For the first time since meeting Chris, I was getting a good look at his body without a layer of clothing getting in the way, and it was nothing short of stunning.

There was still his white, button-up office shirt, but it was so flimsy and thin. It did nothing in terms of keeping his chest hidden from the lust of my eyes.

Taking him from bottom to top again, I bit my bottom lip and said, "Can I take off your pants first?"

He smirked. "Damn, you're really tempting, aren't you?" He said, giving me a hint that he was going to say yes and that I was going to have the chance to take his dick into my mouth right away. "But, no. I took each piece of your clothing at a time, without disrespecting the right order, and I'd like you to do that too."

"You're not making this easy on me," I complained.

"I don't intend to," he joked, widening his smirk.

One button at a time, I undid his office shirt's buttons, revealing more and more of his wide, hairy chest. Pop sounds echoed in the air of his bedroom each time I pulled one button off. His fur, the hair of his chest, made me feel like sliding my hand over it, which I did.

I felt it, cherishing not only his hair, but also the definition of his muscles. It was like he was sculpted to be his way. It was as if before he was born, his mom asked the doctors to let her choose what his appearance was going to be when he became an adult.

I took off his office shirt, my eyes landing on his dilapidated abs. I caressed them with my hand, pressing my fingers, feeling his chest expanding and contracting each time he breathed. His mind was doing everything right now to just not push me with all his strength toward the bed, getting on top of me, and then peppering me with hot, needy kisses.

"What's your next move now?" He asked, keeping himself still and controlled. His muscles twitched a couple of times, reaffirming my previous declaration. He was indeed doing everything in his power to keep his urges in check.

All to make sure I was feeling respected, that he was showing me I was the most important person for him.

"Take off your pants," I said.

"Wrong. Take off my shoes first. You've been allowed to walk in here with just your socks on, but my shoes have the priority right now."

I glanced at one of the chairs by one of the walls of his bedroom, tipping my chin toward it. "Then, sit down."

"And after that, you're going to give me a blowjob?"

I smirked. "We'll see about that."

He proceeded to the chair, plopping down on it, breathing loudly when he spread his legs for me. One shoe at a time, undoing the laces, I took them off him. I sniffed his socks, not finding it surprising that it had a hint of a bad smell, but that for the most part, it tempted me to caress his feet with my tongue.

When he opened his mouth to tell me something, perhaps give me another order, I bit the material of his left sock. Pulling it, I took it off his foot, and then proceeded to do the same with his other sock.

"Damn, you're really tempting me to grab you and bury my cock inside your pussy."

"Are you going to take long to do that?" I questioned, smiling at him as I massaged one of his now bare feet.

"Maybe not," he expressed, turning his head backward and then lifting his hips off the chair. Alright, it was time for me to take them off him. And then, after doing that, the only thing left would be his underwear.

I hoped he was wearing a pair of black, short boxers. They would show the perfection and the definition of his thick legs. He had the thighs of a soccer player- No, they were even better toned than those.

Soccer players all over the world could hold no candle to him.

I undid his belt, pulling it off him, and then tossed it behind me. There was a thud as it fell on the floor, but I didn't pay any attention to it. My eyes were focused on this one thing in front of me: taking off his pants, and then worshipping his baby maker.

Baby? I had no pretensions of making a baby with him, for now, I thought with a dirty, mischievous smile on my face.

I undid the zipper of his pants, settling my fingers underneath the band and then pulling them down. They slid without a hitch, my eyes dawning on his thick and toned legs. If we were in the Summer season, his skin would be a bit more toned than this, looking more tantalizing to the naughty eyes that I had.

But they still looked so erotic, his hair having been trimmed not too long ago. The thickness of his thighs, the sweat trickling down his skin, and the smell of his manliness invading my nostrils – was there anything better than this, more fulfilling and sexier? I couldn't think there was.

Sniffing his underwear, my eyes dawning on the silhouette of his immense cock, I asked, "Can I get to the good part already?"

He quirked up the corners of his lips.

"Of course, my darling."

I couldn't waste any more time, pushing his black boxers down just when he lifted his butt off the padding of the chair, freeing his baby maker. It slipped out, bouncing up and down, a bead of his pre-cum coursing down from his slit.

I flickered my tongue right at the tip of the gland, the smell of his musk feeding my lungs one more time.

He chuckled, my hands caressing his legs. I moved them up, reaching for his low-hanging balls and then kneading them for a second or two. "I thought you were an amateur, Molly, but I'm seeing I was wrong about that."

"Too wrong about it, I'd say," I teased, kissing his balls and then putting one of them into my mouth.

"This whole time, I've been waiting for this," he commented, tilting his head back and allowing me all the freedom I needed.

I took in the sight of him sitting before me, and then wrapped my lips around his gland. My hands didn't let go of his balls, still massaging each of his sperm holders. I kept pressing my fingers against them, applying just the right amount of pressure, and assessing their weight and might.

I bobbed up and down on him for a minute or two, and then took my mouth off it. I didn't take a look at it before kissing the tip of his gland one more time, and then one more time, unsure when this was going to end, if it was going to.

His left eye opened for a fraction of a second, his mind wondering when I was going to go back to doing what I was doing. He didn't need to worry about that for too long. As soon as I was done pressing my fingers on his milk containers, I took the plunge one more time.

This time, I was much more feral, bobbing up and down at great speed, my head nothing more than a blur now. I salivated around his hardness, each time I finished a cycle, all of this getting much easier. I could keep doing this forever and ever, with nothing capable of stopping my handiwork.

"Fucking hell," he murmured, a line of saliva coursing down his mouth.

His words tempted me to go further. I was feeling hotter by the second, putting more of his inches down my throat, deep-throating him. The urge to gag kicked in, but I held it back. A tear rolled down my cheek, but I didn't worry about it.

All the pain was worth the pleasure he was presenting me with.

When his dick twitched, I pulled back. I thought I'd done it in time, but his monster cock erupted. A line of his sperm was shot high in the air, the rest coming out like a water fountain.

Opening his eyes, he said, "There's still more where that's coming from."

I widened my eyes, finding it unbelievable he could cum twice in a row without having to put much effort into it. Chris was just that turned on.

I smirked, flicking my tongue at his gland one more time.

"Then, let's not waste any more time."

"Allow me-" I said, standing up.

But he held his hand up then, freezing me. "First, you're going to clean off my junk. It's pretty dirty, and I know a woman like you can't wait for the chance to taste some of my saltiness on her, or your tongue."

"You read my mind," I affirmed, getting back on my knees and licking his dick from base to top. His girth was tempting, the accompanying length even more so. Veins bulged out on his baby maker, the saltiness of his discharge more tempting than anything I'd experienced before.

When he was clean, he pushed me to the bed, getting himself on top of me. His dilapidated, immense body loomed over me, making me gasp as shivers ran down my spine. It was one thing mentioning the fact we should be doing this, and another to have him do it.

His hand pressed and played with my folds, his lips parting. "You're so wet right now. I'm going to get in there and I'm not going to pull out. Are you okay with that, or do you think I should put a condom on first?"

I brushed my nails down his back. "No, condom, please. I don't want anything getting in the way."

"As you wish," he purred just when I wrapped my legs around him, pulling myself up to his hardness.

The head of his penis touched my pussy. Settling his fingers underneath my thighs, he pulled me to him with all his strength, getting inside me in one go. Pain flared through me, but it still didn't deter me from bathing myself in all the pleasure he was presenting me with.

I moaned, groaning. His strokes were slow and measured at the beginning, but soon he picked up the pace. "I'm going to shoot my seed inside you, baby girl. You have no problem with that, do you?"

I shook my head. "No problem at all. Make me come. Shoot your load inside me. I need all of it."

"Damn, you're so slutty right now," he purred, rolling his hips, pistoning in and out, ramming me with all his might.

It took him no time at all then, his rod twitching one more time, erupting inside me. His milk, creamy and hot, overflooded my pussy. And he hadn't lied. He kept his promise, tainting me with his sperm.

The smell of sex and sweat filled the air, his body plopping down beside me. He'd pulled out, making me feel a little lost and exposed. His arms wrapping around me, soon reaffirmed his commitment to me, though.

Yes, he'd possibly just made me pregnant. I wasn't on birth control. I didn't want to take any pills. After spending so much time waiting for the right man, wondering if he would ever show up or not, I guessed it was finally time to settle down.

And what better choice for that than Christopher Sheppard?

EPILOGUE

Christopher

The sun was blaring its light on us, making me tip up my sunglasses. I stole a look at the women walking around on the sand, perambulating here and there, but they were quite disappointing in their beauty. No one came close to the piece of pure gorgeousness lounging beside me, her eyes also covered by a pair of big and round sunglasses.

She had just her bikini on, showing most of her skin to other men on the beach. They dared to steal looks at her, but they didn't last more than a couple of seconds. And there was a very good reason behind that, of course.

I was keeping watch. Nobody could ever think they could have a claim on her. Molly was my woman.

The shine of the ring on her finger also informed lesser men of her marital status. She'd been married to me for five years now.

Lounging beside me was our little kid. Our little kiddo, as we liked to call him. His blond hair reminded him of me, but his eyes, so big and expressive, brought memories associated with Molly.

He was a man with a capital M and his hair was blond, but the rest of his being, his body, reminded me of Molly.

His mother took a sip from her coconut water, straight from a coconut itself, putting it down. She propped her head on the large floral pillow, exhaling air from her tantalizing and beautiful bust.

If it weren't against the laws, I'd be making love with her right here and now. I just couldn't be bothered about the consequences of such a frivolous thing, in that case.

"Is there something bothering you right now, my love?"

"No, I'm just thinking about the past."

"Thinking about the past, really? Any specific incident in mind?"

"How we met, for starters."

"You still think that was odd? I would never have abandoned someone like you."

"Maybe it was just because I'm the most beautiful woman in the whole world?"

She smirked, joking about that. She might as well be.

"I don't know," I answered, quirking up a corner of my lips too. "There are a lot of women that could compete with you in that regard."

She widened her smile at my joke, certain I was doing nothing more than that.

Even though her kind of body wasn't the one most women sought, she was proud of it. No fat shaming there, and either way, I didn't see her under such scrutinization. I saw her as a woman who needed love, to be worshipped, and treated with the respect her Queen origins deserved.

Even now, lying on this beach bed, my dick was beginning to get hard. I didn't want someone noticing that, but if they did, then I wouldn't be able to care less.

I was with the woman of my life, and I had a nice little kiddo that could behave himself. He could be throwing a tantrum right now, yelling that he'd rather be in his house, playing with his friends, and the like.

But he was cool with this. He was cool with us just relaxing on the beach, burning away all the stress that came with running my own company.

He was sipping his orange juice from the glass, his eyes also covered by a pair of sportsy, red sunglasses. He looked cool, the front of his hair combed up. The sides were cut shorter than the top, giving him a playboy look.

He was such a smart little kid, especially for someone his age.

"You want to go with me into the water?" Molly asked, standing up.

I stood up, responding, "Of course, what else would I be doing right now without you?"

Lloyd put down on the small, round table his orange juice, doing so with enough force to make some of it splash out of the glass. "Hey, I want to go with!"

He had just a pair of soft blue, floral shorts on. Even though he was wearing his sunglasses, I could perceive the intensity of his stare at us. Most of all, he didn't want to be left alone. And he didn't need to worry about that. Even before saying to Molly I was going with her into the ocean's sloshing water, I was already thinking about inviting him to go with us.

I rubbed his hair, messing it up. "Of course, kiddo. You didn't really think we were going to keep you here all alone, did you?"

"Well, I could never know with you two," he complained, crossing his arms over his small, skinny chest.

I grabbed his hand. "Want me to teach you a thing or two about swimming?"

He was pouting, remembering that his friends weren't nearby to bully him about that. They all knew how to swim at their age, so he'd been bothering me about me teaching him that for months now. I guessed it was finally time to begin his classes.

His pouting ceased to be, his expression softening up.

"Okay, daddy. Then, teach me how to swim! I want to show everyone in class I can swim too."

"And, I'm going to help you," Molly said, grabbing his other hand.

Lloyd's cheeks flushed all of sudden. "You're both making me feel that I'm just a little boy right now."

"But you are," I insisted, taking him to the beach. "You're my little kiddo. You don't have to prove to your friends anything. They know you're better than them."

He smiled.

Molly smiled.

We were living the life.

The End

Thank you for the reception for my previous books. Writing BBW Alpha Male is something that always excites me, and it's so great to know there's a whole audience hungry for that kind of story.

As one last little thing, I'd like to request you to leave a review for this book on the Amazon store page (or just how many stars you think it deserves). It doesn't take long, and your opinion is very valuable to me. I know some of you leave your reviews on Goodreads, but on Amazon is where they have more visibility, and you'd be helping me a lot, too.

OTHER BOOKS BY JOLIE DAMMAN

Venom Curves: A BBW Alpha Male Romance
Impossibly Curvy: A BBW Alpha Male
Wild Curves: A Western BBW Alpha Male Instalove Romance
Unfair Curves: A BBW Alpha Male Romance Bundle
Mafia Vassal: A Dark Italian Mafia Romance Bundle
Beg Me: An Arranged Marriage Dark Mafia Romance
Don't Cry: A Secret Baby Dark Mafia Romance
Seizing her Heart: A Bratva Mafia Romance Collection
Conquering my Queen: A Dark Mafia Romance Bundle
Challenging Destiny: An Arranged Marriage Dark Mafia Romance
Chaining my Queen: A Secret Baby Dark Mafia Romance
Hell is Crying: A Secret Baby Mafia Romance
Beyond Forgiving: A Dark Mafia Captive Romance
Chosen to be Mine: A Dark Arranged Marriage Mafia Romance
Have no Fear: An Enemies to Lovers Academy Romance
Under his Mercy: A Dark High School Bully Romance
Lure Me: A Dark High School Bully Romance
Fallen Angel: A Dark High School Bully Romance
Stop Lying: A Dark High School and College Bundle
Stop Running: A Dark High School Bully Romance
Take Control: A Dark High School Bully Romance

ABOUT THE AUTHOR

Jolie Damman lives with her puppies and many cats on her farmland. She enjoys spending time with nature and tending to her property. When she has some free time, which doesn't happen as often as she would like, she writes her books.

As a writer, she hopes to touch and change the heart of her readers. Her books are not for those weak of the heart, and they tend to be spicier than most. One word after the other, she doesn't stop typing until she has written her idea, and she is very desire-driven when it comes to establishing the connections of her characters.